CHROMARIA

Clayton Demera

To my wife, my two sons, and my Siberian husky, where most of the ideas for this storyline were found on our many walks together.

Table of Contents

ACKNOWLEDGEMENTS

I would like to express my deepest gratitude to my mother, Loretta, my father-in-law, Richard, and last but not least my wife, Rachel, for being the first to read and proofread this book. Their keen eyes and honest feedback were invaluable in shaping the final manuscript. I am forever grateful for their unwavering support and encouragement throughout this journey.

I also want to acknowledge American Publisher for their professional guidance and assistance in bringing this book to life. Their expertise in the publishing process made this dream a reality, and I am incredibly thankful for their partnership.

ABOUT THE AUTHOR

Clayton, a father of two, always had a passion for storytelling. While attempting to create a digital asset, he rekindled his creative fire and embarked on writing his greatest creation yet. This book marks the beginning of an exciting series, with seven more installments to follow. Balancing family life and his love for writing, Clayton crafts compelling narratives that captivate readers of all ages.

1.   IN THE BEGINNING

In the beginning, there was The Creator. The world was not yet filled, and the Creator said, "Let there be light," and it was so. This was the creation of the first tribe, 'The Yellow Tribe.' Yellow would control the season cycles and the weather of the land.

The beginning continued, the Creator said, "Let the waters have life," and the second tribe was created, 'The Blue Tribe.' This tribe would control the water, how it spreads through the land, and the properties of it.

The beginning continued further as now the land appeared and the third tribe was created called 'The Orange Tribe.' They would control the ground and be the builders of castles in the kingdom.

The Creator said, "Let there be growth through vegetation and fruit-yielding trees with seeds in it," and the fourth tribe was created, 'The Green Tribe.' They worked and controlled the plant life of the world.

The beginning persisted and the Creator said, "Let the land and waters bring forth wildlife that swim, fly, and roam the land." This was the fifth tribe, 'The Red Tribe.' This tribe would control wildlife with assistance from birth, life, and death.

Then the beginning continued with the Creator making a large mountain. This would be the region closest to him and the sixth tribe was created, 'The Purple Tribe.' This tribe would be the spirit tribe and would be blessed to be close to the Creator. This tribe would provide guidance to the land.

The beginning was complete and the Creator was satisfied. Out of his abundant love for his creation, he created the final tribe, 'The Indigo Tribe.' This tribe would serve the people. All tribes would provide hospitality and in return they would give entertainment, music, humor, shows, and wonders to mystify the tribes.

When the creator was finished, he took a drop of blood from each of the first tribe members and on that holy day he blessed them. The blood rose to the sky and a great rainbow was cast above the creation.

The creator spoke to the tribes and said, "I have set the colors in the sky as a covenant between the tribes and me. Let it be a reminder of the harmony between the tribes and the kingdom in which I gave you."

The Purple Tribe was taken to the top of the mountain, and for seven cycles they were given instructions on holy obligations that the tribes needed to do to keep favor with the creator.

When a child is born to a tribe, a celebration must occur within seven cycles. The baby must be held high at this celebration and a prick of their finger showing the color of the blood must be recognized.

When a tribe member passes away from the creation, a ceremony of worship must be held by two other tribesmen. A prick of his blood must be taken and the words saying, "Creator in your abundance of love and rich in mercy, please let this tribesman return to his color above with you."

Finally, on every 700th cycle, all tribes will meet at the base of the Divine Mountain. The Indigo Tribe will provide seven cycles of entertainment for the worship ceremonies. This will be the declaration to the Creator of all tribe's obedience and submission.

For each cycle at Divine Mountain, one tribe member from each tribe would present an offering to the Creator. This offering will be kept with the Purple Tribe and then placed at the base of Divine Mountain.

These covenants were made and delivered to each tribe in a stone tablet. It was to be kept at the leader's quarters of each tribe. This was a symbol of the Creator and his overwhelming love.

From this moment on, The Creator did not speak to the tribes directly. The Purple Tribe honored the

Chromaria

Creator and signs were given. But direct contact with the Creator ended. It is believed everything was given and no further direct involvement was needed.

At the top of all the stone tablets laid the name of an unknown creation, "Chromaria."

As the cycles happened the tribes committed to the covenant established by the Creator. Over time, animals were born and raised, plants grew and yielded fruits and vegetables. The earth was used to build castles for each of the tribes. The rains came and snow fell and melted.

Entertainment occurred throughout each of the tribes by the Indigo Tribe. Music was played, jokes were told, and performances were done which left the children in awe.

The Purple Tribe on every 700th cycle told the other tribes of signs they saw, heard, or felt. Continuously encouraging the other tribes to trust the Creator and observe the rainbow as a sign of his love for us. Above all else the most important thing in the life given by the Creator was to observe his covenants.

The cycles carried on, and the Orange Tribe assisted other tribes in developing and building their castles. The leader's quarters were designed to reflect each tribe's special purpose given by the Creator. However, each castle had special quarters only the Indigo Tribe were allowed to occupy during their visits.

The Yellow Tribe established four different seasons for Chromaria. The first was the Sow Season, which indicated the season to establish crops. The Grow Season, was when the plants once sprouted and would grow in the heat of the land. The Harvest Season was the season where the tribes would reap the land. Finally, the Rest Season, the coldest of all the seasons, where all tribes would rest more than work. The seasons could only change by the Yellow Tribe having a cycle of fasting.

The Blue Tribe controlled the waters and worked with the changing seasons. They built dams, bridges, and provided river paths to assist other tribes. They also had a day of fasting (they would not eat) to enrich the minerals of the water to help plants grow. This provides nutrients to the tribes when they drank from it.

The Green and Red tribes assisted the growth of plants and animals. They were very close and had a fast every season to ensure their yield was enough to provide for all tribes.

For the animals would eat the plant life and the Green Tribe would benefit from a healthy harvest of the animals.

Now some animals were considered wild and not used for the harvest. An ecosystem existed and needed to be maintained by the red tribe.

They would give balance to the animals to avoid overgrazing or possible attacks on tribe members by predators.

The Green Tribe also had a relationship with the Orange Tribe. They would meet at the end of the rest season. A feast called the 'Growth Feast' was held between the two and the Orange Tribe would give guidance on where the balance was in the soil. The guidance was taken to plant certain items in areas for the best results.

This balance in structure was a fourth blessing given by the Creator. The only way harmony existed was through mutual teamwork and observing the covenants.

2.   FAITH IN THE RAINBOW

The seasons came, and the cycles continued. All the covenants were held, and the balance between the tribes was maintained.

However, during the 21st Grow Season, the Blue Tribe was working on a tributary of the Crystal River. The river was becoming much stronger in current and required a release to a low-lying area. While working on the river, the ferocious current of the stream engulfed his hardworking son, who was a growing man getting old year by year. It was his only son and his wife had passed on to the rainbow a couple of cycles ago.

The son was strong for his age and soon, within the next few seasons, would be on his own outside his father's home. His son was ambitious and wanted to be part of the process.

The son got into the water by the river's edge to work on clearing the area. The father approved of this and went to the other side of the river to do the same.

The current was strong however the two men continued to work. The father was close to completion of his side; he started to smile. He looked up assuming his son was close to completion too, but he didn't see him in his spot.

In a flurry of emotions, he ran to the other side only to see his son downriver with his head down next to a tree motionless.

He ran to his son to check on him, but it was too late. He had passed away. His spirit returned to the rainbow. The father took him into the woods and buried him but forgot to include two other tribesmen and a place of worship at his burial.

During the 168th sow Season, an elder—late in her years woman from the Purple Tribe was about to have a child. Her husband was at the base of one of the seven prayer mountain peaks. They spent seven cycles at the base in meditation.

On the third cycle of meditation the child was born, and the mother passed away a day later. Upon the elder's return he found the child and was told she lived two extra days. He assumed the blood prick was done, but it did not happen.

On the 336th Harvest season, a great storm occurred. This was the cycle right before the 700th cycle. The Orange tribal land was completely flooded, and their travel abilities were hampered. They arrived at the base of the mountain on the 702nd cycle.

All these events happened and caused the covenants to be broken, yet nothing changed. The Creator did not bring forth great destruction. The primary covenant the tribes considered most important is during the death of their people and returning them to the rainbow.

Over time the Creator was forgotten but the rainbow above was not. The submission and obedience for the gatherings at the base of every 700th cycle were now given unto the rainbow. The blood oath to the child was for connecting the child to the rainbow and not the Creator.

Finally, the return to the rainbow for the dead became the most important event. Even the children were taught not about the Creator but rather the rainbow itself.

The Purple Tribe was the most troubled by this change. They made a grave mistake of fearing revolt from the tribes themselves rather than the wrath of the Creator.

The Purple Tribe began to state their meditation was to get close to the rainbow and not the Creator.

The Creator is abundant with love and mercy. Justice is not obtained by force but by divine inspiration.

While the balance remained in the tribes, a lack of belief in the Creator as the true source of all things resulted in a conflict that would be introduced.

The conflict would allow each tribe to look individually into their souls. They would be given an opportunity to seek what is truly in their hearts.

A great storm began in the middle of the Harvest Season and began to cover all Chromaria. The Purple Tribe began to worship at the base of the mountain in fear of why such a large storm was brewing from the rainbow.

The storm did not produce any rain. It was dark, windy and with loud thunder. But it had seventy distinct lightning strikes. These strikes were swords sent from beyond the rainbow. They pierced through the rainbow and landed all over Chromaria.

3.   A CONFLICT IS INTRODUCED

These swords were foreign to the tribes because fighting was considered unnecessary. The tribes needed to work together to establish balance and maintain their way of life.

Three tribesmen from the Orange Tribe found three swords. They felt the power and one said, "We don't need balance with these, we can take what we want. If anyone tries to stop us, we can slay them and send them to the rainbow. For we control the ground. The domains everyone lives in, are by our hands. We are the best tribe."

The power flowed through their bodies. Their souls, with swords in hand, felt violence could be useful. They knew the Green Tribe held the most wealth and power during the harvest Season. The three-headed towards the Green Tribe's current location.

During the harvest, an elder named Anu and his son Manu were working in the field called the Great Plain of Mercy. Manu was a young adolescent. He loved his father, who was loved by all his tribe.

Anu was behaving anxiously, and Manu asked if he was sick. He told Manu, "No, I just heard some scary stories about the Orange Tribe. They might have broken the balance between the tribes."

Manu in his curiosity asked, "What do you mean, are they not listening to the Creator?"

Anu replied, "We know very few still listen to the Creator already, but this feels different. The storm last night also felt different."

In the distance marched a small group of Yellow tribesmen. Manu sees this group and thinks nothing of it. However, his eyebrow rose, and he looked up again. They are much closer and moving quickly, he then notices something. He asks his father, "What are the Yellow tribesmen carrying and what is on their face?"

Anu walks over and looks and sees Indigo blood on their faces and they are all carrying a sword. His heart sunk; he knew something was very wrong. He looked at Manu and said, "Son, I want you to listen to me, run into the field and hide. Do not come out till you hear my whistle."

Manu replied, "Yes Father." As Anu stood up after instructing his son, he was struck by one of the Yellow tribesmen across his head. This frightened Manu and he ran away as fast as he could. He looked back and while not paying attention, he tripped over a rock. His face planted in the dirt. He looked up at something shining in front of him. It was the same type of weapon the Yellow tribesmen had, a sword.

Manu grabbed it and the first thought that rushed into his head was, *I can help and protect my father.* He ran back towards his father and as he came out of the crops, he saw him on the ground.

A Yellow tribesman with his back to Manu was blocking his vision. Manu ran up and struck the tribesman, knocking the tribesman's sword out of his hand. The swords were touching each other on the ground and a bright light shined in both, then they became one.

The tribesman over Anu said, "The swords become stronger together, but we are the first of the Creator's creation. All must bow to us," and then he struck Anu with a deathblow.

Manu screamed in agony. His heart filled with rage and right before he rushed the group, a Blue tribeswoman jumped over him and began to throw rocks at the Yellow tribesman. She looked at Manu and said, "We must run and retreat now!" Then they ran and hid in the crops in the Great Plain.

A father and son in the Red Tribe named Ando and Sando were feeding their cattle. Ando loved his son; he was the strongest and brightest of the younger generation. He also had compassion for the weak, which was a good trait in tending animals. But he was still young and a child, with a promising future.

Ando told his son he needed more feed for the cattle and would be right back as he walked to the barn. He looked over many bags of feed, found the right one and picked it up. He then heard a scream from his son.

He dropped the bag and ran back towards his son, worried one of the cattle might have stepped on him causing an injury. But as he returned, he saw three Orange Tribesmen standing over his son. His life was taken, and the men were killing the cattle.

Ando—a strong man, boiled with anger. If his son had been killed, then his life was a feeling of meaningless now. He screamed "NO" and ran towards the men. He punched one in the face, and he fell to the ground. He got on top and continued to strike the man in a blind rage.

As the other two Orange tribesmen came to help, one swung their sword at Ando. He ducked, counterstroke with a punch and disarmed the sword. He then took that sword and ended the life of the three tribesmen.

He ran over to his son Sando and grabbed his body, emotions flared in him as he held him. He started to cry saying, "You can't be gone; no this isn't happening." A rage built inside of him, as if he could see the color, red. He was hyperventilating and foaming at the mouth in anger. He felt a change, but not inside of him but rather in Chromaria.

Then an eerie silence occurred as if everything stopped: the wind, the grass, and all the animals were staring at him. Then a whisper fell on Ando's ears saying…

"You should be upset about your son. You loved him deeply. Someone should pay for this injustice done unto you."

This whisper felt cold but like a blanket around him. A thought-like feeling but had a presence other than my own.

Ando agreed with the voice. He said, "Someone will pay for my son's death." He looked around at all the swords that laid on the ground by the dead tribesmen.

The voice came again, "Those swords have power. Power to help you in your quest for revenge. Together they gain strength, like the old-world tribes."

Ando said, "Old-world? Has our way of life changed?"

The voice responded, "Your son's life has changed."

Ando asked, "What are you?" "I am the unseen, the out of your reach, unknown, the mysterious, enigmatically obscure I am—" the voice replied.

"You are the Darkness," said Ando.

4.   TO SEE OR NOT TO SEE

Manu and the girl ran and found a large rock inside the Great Plain where they stopped. Exhausted and confused Manu asked while trying to catch his breath, "What… why… who are you first of all?"

She replied also out of breath, "I am Udo, from the Blue Tribe. I have been on the run since my father was killed by the same tribe that attacked you."

Manu asked, "What happened to your father?"

Udo explained her father found a sword himself and told Udo and her mother he was going to travel for a day. I followed him in secret. While he traveled with two of his work partners, he… he attacked an Orange tribesman.

The three that attacked you took his life. I ran and hid for some time. Eventually following the Orange Tribe, that is when I found you.

Suddenly, Manu heard a voice, "Son you must continue to run." Manu jumps up and sees his father, but he is transparent.

Manu says, "Father, what are you now? Why are you here?!"

Udo looking confused asks, "What are you doing, are you talking to me?"

He looks at his father and starts crying and says, "Father why can't she see you and why… why are you here and not—"

His father interrupts him, "Up there," and points to the rainbow above.

Anu says, "I am not sure; this must be a part of the Creator's plan. I am here with you for now."

Manu explains to Udo what he is seeing and is not sure why his father did not return to the rainbow. Udo also wonders why she was not able to see her father now when he passed, did he return to the rainbow or is he gone forever she wondered. From there they ran into the Dark Woods to be more concealed and hidden.

Meanwhile Ando's plan was simple, the tribe that killed his son was the tribe he wanted to destroy. The Darkness wanted Ando to not worry about simple things such as who was the Darkness. The primary focus was the pain, and how to find revenge from it.

Ando knew a large structure was being built, a dam. He knew the Orange Tribe was bringing large rocks towards the mouth of the Crystal River.

He found a caravan of many different carts being pulled toward this area. As he crouched down in the tall grass to watch them, he saw another sword on the ground.

He touched it with the sword he had, and it became one, it glowed like a bolt of lightning. He asked the Darkness, "How many swords exist?"

The Darkness whispered, "The question is not how many exist but how many will fulfill your plan of redemption? How many will make the Creator suffer for what he has caused you to grieve for?"

The Darkness continued, "The Creator put a hole in your heart. Only justice for your son's death will fill the hole."

Ando asked, "The hole you speak of, is painful. How will I fill it?"

The Darkness replied, "Oh I think you know the answer, but I will give you a hint. Conquering the land, taking from the weaker tribes that didn't experience your pain. Show them where the power belongs—in your heart."

Ando looked at the caravan and said, "I will start with them." He ran towards the group and within a short period, he took the life of all except three of the strongest. He offered them a higher rank than the Creator gave them.

The Darkness suggested, "Building an empire to serve you will not be easy. But maybe taking from the yield of the land will also add to your power."

Ando replied, "Let's move towards the Green Tribe's land."

5.   DREAMS AND POWER

Udo and Manu found an area to sleep for the cycle.

Udo stated, "We will sleep well next to the river. The water will make us calm." Manu agreed and both went to sleep quickly.

Manu closed his eyes and woke up to a rising sun. He heard the river water flowing. He sat up and looked to his left at the river. His heart struck with fear, and he stood up quickly. The entire river was red, filled with blood.

He woke up and realized he was having a nightmare. His father still close to him yet far away whispered, "You must keep going, your journey grows in importance by the cycle."

Manu quickly woke up Udo and explained the dream. Udo thought about it and asked, "Do you think the Creator is punishing us? I mean neither of us followed the covenant for our fathers when they died. Yet neither returned to the rainbow and I can't even speak or see my father's spirit."

Manu looked down and took a deep breath. He then said looking down, "Our creator is rich in mercy; his love knows no bounds." Manu walks toward a large tree and touches it with his palm. He continued, "We have many questions, but where should we seek answers?"

Udo responds, "If we seek answers about the Creator then the answer is simple: we must head to the Spirit Tribe. Since the harvest time is now, we know the Indigo Tribe will also be near the base of the mountain."

Manu knew the Spirit and Purple were interchangeable terms and replied, "Let us get going then, I will protect you. Unless we find another sword which you can use."

Udo replied, "I will never use the weapon that caused my father's death!"

Meanwhile, Ando is standing on a small cliff looking over the land of Chromaria. Behind him is a small contingency of mixed tribesmen he has developed. He has quickly combined fourteen swords, and the men see him as a king. Ando sees small signs of the land and it is decaying. The instability now appears to have an impact on the land.

The Darkness whispers to Ando, "Why does your Creator hate you? Look what the Creator has done to the land, the people, and your son. The swords give you power but the people give you strength. Your pain gives you purpose, but your creator only takes from you."

Ando turns around and faces the men following him. He raises his sword, and they cheer him on. He begins a small speech to the men.

"Your Creator gave you this world in rich abundance for you. But his last gift was the sword. These swords symbolize change. Each tribe now thinks they are the Creator's favorite. Truth is the Creator has forsaken you. Follow me, for I will give you a new life, a new purpose, and a new King of Chromaria!"

The small contingency cheers the king on! They begin to chant, "ANDO! ANDO!"

The Darkness whispered to Ando, "They will serve their purpose well. Above all your glory will matter most."

Ando smiled and said, "I would like to be entertained." He turned to the group and said, "Who wants a night of entertainment!?" The group cheered him on. Ando replied, "We will march to the mountain base; there we will find the Indigo Tribe."

Ando looks back over the cliff and sees the Valley of Truth leading to Divine Mountain. He smiles and says, "I know the way! Follow me!"

6.   SING TO ME

As they walk further towards the mountain base, Udo stops and picks up a few rocks. She puts them in her pocket, looks at Manu and says, "I will defend myself with Chromaria, not what has fallen here."

Manu walks up to Udo and gently grabs her forearm and asks, "Do you hear that?"

It was a musical sound and Udo knew right away. She smiled and said, "It is the Indigo!"

She ran to the top of a small hill. Looking in the distance was the tribe, but they were marching away from the base of the Divine Mountain.

Manu said, "This is strange, if we hurry, we can cut them off. We should stop them and see why they are leaving the base."

Udo replied, "Alright but leave your sword in the large bush by the road there so you don't scare them."

They both ran down the hill to a small pathway the Indigo Tribe were taking. Manu set his sword in a bush right by the pathway where he could see it.

As the parade saw them in the middle of the pathway, they slowed down.

Now the Indigo Tribe is rooted in entertainment. Meaning other than providing songs, plays, tricks and magic, they are somewhat difficult to deal with. Trying to talk to them is like speaking to a musical instrument.

As they ran in front of the tribe, they put both their hands up and said, "We like music, we like dance, please, please just one chance." This was what children would say when the Indigo would arrive for entertainment.

The whole tribe begins to move back and forth, an elder hops off the back of a carriage. His robe was beautiful and glittered in color. He bobbed his head and moved as if he was dancing.

The Elder states, "I am Fasola, you must move, for we must go. We are in a rush and have no time for a show."

Manu replied, "We just have one question for you."

The tribe stopped moving and Fasola took a step back.

Udo whispered to Manu, "You have to sing; you cannot talk directly to them."

Manu looking confused began to ask again, "Ahh… ok. Well… um… this is different, this is strange, why has your destination changed?"

The tribe began to move again, and the Elder said, "We must go, for we must hide, for the power of the mountain is about what is inside."

Manu started moving back and forth like the tribe and said, "Inside. Inside I must see, what's in the mountain, could you please tell me?"

Udo looked at Manu and smiled as she was impressed at how he was adapting to the conversation. The elder danced and spun around. He then pointed to the bush where Manu laid his sword.

He said, "In the bush you have two, what to do oh what to do, but go and see, yes go and see, for the true power is within all three."

Manu grabs Udo's arm and says, "We should go, it sounds like a third sword is there and it will combine with mine!"

She stares at the elder and shakes off Manu and says, "Wait!"

She looked down and said, "I am sad, so so sad, how come I can't but he can see his dad?"

The elder put his hand on her shoulder and said, "Some swords are good, and some are bad but trust in the Creator's purpose is all we have."

Then suddenly out of the woods walked Ando with his small army. The army grabbed many of the tribesmen and walked up to the elder looked deep into his eyes and said, "Now sing me a song."

7.   A DIFFERENT SWORD

Manu and Udo stood behind a wagon, kneeled, and watched Ando speak with the elder.

Manu tells Udo, "I feel strange."

Udo responds, "What is the matter?"

He replies, "I feel, I really need to get back to the bush and get my sword."

Ando while holding the elder's neck, presses his sword on his cheek. A small drip of blood falls and Ando asks, "Why are you leaving the mountain?"

The elder does not answer and just stares at Ando. One of Ando's soldiers yells, "You have to sing it to them!"

Ando begins to press the sword harder on the elder's face and whispers, "Do I?"

Ando submits and says, "Ok, tell me now, this is not a trick, what is in the mountain? Tell me or you will die quick!"

The elder begins to move back and forth and says, "Your sword is close but so is another, first to get to the mountain will defeat the other."

Manu looks at Udo and says, "I am going to run to my sword, we will need it to defend ourselves. Make a distraction for me."

Udo agrees and pulls a small stone from her pocket, she says, "GO!"

She stands up and Manu runs, Ando sees him and throws the elder to the ground. He takes one step towards Manu but is hit in the eye with a stone from Udo.

Ando begins to march towards Udo. Udo starts throwing stones at different soldiers. One on her left, one on her right, and one behind her. Manu gets back to the bush and grabs his sword.

He hears his father whisper to him, "Protect Udo."

Manu stands up and says, "I will Father." Manu turns around and sees Udo throwing rocks at the soldiers, but Ando is right behind her.

Manu screams, "Udo look out!"

She turns around and Ando is right there and thrusts his sword into her stomach. She gasps, her eyes wide open.

Ando leans in and asks, "Where is your father?"

Udo turns her head slightly and, in the distance, she sees her father watching her. He is in the same form as Manu said he saw his father, as a spirit. His face is sad, ashamed of what he is witnessing.

A tear begins to fall down her eye and Ando pushes the sword in further to finish the job. She falls to the ground and takes her last breath.

Manu yells in heartbreaking pain, "NO!"

Ando turns his head and tells the soldiers, "Get him." Three rush Manu and one by one they swing their swords at him. Each one cracks when it strikes his. Manu in defense cuts each soldier's leg and impales them.

Ando out of frustration walks over to Manu and lifts his sword as Manu appears to be an easy target that got extremely lucky with his three soldiers. His sword strikes Manu's, and a shock wave explodes. Both stand in amazement. Manu takes a small step back and runs into the woods.

Ando out of confusion and frustration goes back to the elder. He grabs him by his robe and looks into his eyes. The elder shaking in fear awaits his next move.

"You see this sword, this sword in my hand. How can I make it the most powerful sword in all of the land?"

The elder stands up and says, "You must find only one more to max your power, but so does another to have a strong tower."

The Darkness whispers to Ando, "The child has a powerful sword like yours, but you must get to Divine Mountain first. He will try to take your glory."

Ando smiles and looks at the elder. He says, "No more songs," and takes his sword and strikes Fasola, taking his life. Ando then absorbs the dead tribesmen's swords. Then looks to his remaining soldiers and says, "We head to the mountain!"

8.   SEEING THE LIGHT

Manu runs as fast as he can deep into the Dark Woods. He stops at a large tree and catches his breath. Overwhelmed with emotion he begins to cry. He drops on his knees, holds his sword with both hands and closes his eyes.

"Creator, why must I endure such suffering?" he asks. All he hears are the birds singing in the woods.

"You must keep going, Son," Manu hears. His father encouraging him in a time of pain. "You must keep going till the end," the father states in a cryptic tone. "The creator will provide direction if you trust in his mercy and love."

Manu looks down while kneeling. Feeling defeated, he takes a deep breath and stands up. He looks behind him and sees no one followed him into the woods.

Manu then looks forward and sees a peculiar sight. Out of all the trees which all have green leaves, one is bright yellow. His father's words echo in his mind.

Manu begins to walk toward the tall yellow tree. His speed increases as does his curiosity of the anomaly. As he gets closer, he notices some of the bushes are covered in frost.

He then sees a sword waving back and forth. Manu holds his own sword in a defensive manner and gets closer. Finally, he sees a young boy sitting with his legs crossed. He is holding the sword upright and swaying it back and forth.

Before Manu can say anything, the boy says, "I like the Harvest season. What say you?"

Manu tells, "I find joy in all seasons the creator allows me to live in."

The boy says, "My name is Ernte. I am of the first, the light, the Yellow Tribe." Ernte holds his sword in the air as he is speaking proudly.

"Do you know the gift our tribe was given?" Ernte asks. Before Manu can answer the boy stands up looking into the sky and says, "We are given a special task in life. Mine was challenging. I am supposed to find the most important item ever."

Manu looks at him confused. He asks, "That seems vague, what item do you mean?"

Ernte responds, "I believe it is this sword I am holding. But do you know what the most important task is that I must do?" He pauses then says, "I have to give it away."

He turns to Manu and points his sword at him. Manu raises his sword, and the handle gets warm. The swords touch and a flash occurs, one sword remains. Ernte looks at Manu and smiles. He says, "My life goal is complete; I think you know what you need to do next."

Manu replies, "Thank you, I must head to Divine Mountain."

Ando, however, is already at the base of the mountain. He has three Spirit Tribe members on their knees in front of him. He says to the Purple Tribe members, "I will make this easy for you, tell me how my sword can obtain the most power and I might let you live."

The youngest stands up and says, "My name is Justo and the answer to your question is simple. You need to merge the most swords."

Ando looks around and says, "Is that all?"

The boy responds and says, "Well three are special, those three can protect the best but are not of the power of the Creator."

Ando asks, "One last question, can this protective sword defeat the power sword?"

Justo responds, "Our Creator does keep some knowledge outside of us. It is for our own protection."

Ando responds, "Very well, how about you join him then!" He chops down the young boy with his sword.

He then turns to his soldiers and says, "It is the end of the line for you." He takes their lives and combines all their swords. He is now ready to enter Divine Mountain.

When the swords of his soldiers combined with his sword the color changed. The sword itself became a deep blue color for a moment. Then two number sixes flashed on both sides of the sword.

"You are very close in power. The creator seems to have dropped a certain number, a total of swords. If you take the three the boy has and the sixty-six you have now, then we are at sixty-nine total. The last one must be inside Mount Divine which makes seventy. Very clever of him," says the Darkness.

"Well, I shall get the last sword then," said Ando.

9.   DIVINE MOUNTAIN

Divine Mountain has two entrances. Ando at the base entered below. Manu peeks through a bush. He sees the slain soldiers that followed Ando. Sad, he looks down. He looks to his right and his father has his hand on his shoulder.

"You must finish my son, take the other entrance to the Cavern of Gifts," his dad tells him.

Manu stands up and walks out of the bush. He stops and turns around. Facing his father, he points his sword up and says, "To the end, Father!"

His father is deeply proud of how far his son has come and grown up with so much trauma he has experienced. His father responds, "The Creator is rich in mercy, remember that Son."

Manu runs to the side of Divine Mountain. The entrance is smaller, the size for a young man to enter. As he crawls inside it becomes very dark. But a glimmer of light shows the end of the small tunnel.

Manu crawls out the end and a large cavern with a staircase going to the top of the mountain. A ray of light shines in the cavern from above. It is shining right on a sword. The whole cavern is beautiful. Fully orchestrated with all the gifts given as an offering to the Creator over time. This sword was sticking up in the muddy center in some water. The water was not very deep.

Meanwhile, Ando walks into the base of the cave and sees a prayer area with candles. He grabs one of the lit candles to go deep into the top of the cave.

"The boy must not reach the last sword before you. He represents everything you have lost with your son. The creator mocks your pain," the Darkness whispers to Ando.

The Darkness continues, "This is your glory to take. You are so close but so far away."

As Ando walks deeper into the cave, he also sees the light. He begins to walk into the Cavern of Gifts. He notices the area in which his tribe laid gifts. For a moment he remembers his son with him at the last 700th celebration. He hears a sound and looks towards the center and sees the boy standing in front of the sword. The boy holds his sword in the air and yells at Ando, "To the end!"

Ando's anger ignites knowing this boy had the audacity to think he could stand before him, and dare say anything aggressive.

"To your end, boy," Ando smiles as he points his sword at Manu.

Ando takes one step forward and the whole mountain rattles. He loses his balance but regains it. Manu and Ando look around startled at what just happened. Then a flash of light shines from the top of the stairs. Both turn and look.

The light became so bright you couldn't see, then it stopped and there he was. The Creator himself. In all his majesty.

Manu was frozen, in awe. The only action Manu could do was to kneel, so he did.

The beauty was indescribable, incomprehensible, imagine all the beauty he's ever seen put together in one moment. In a living being in front of him. The Creator was all white, as if all the colors combined in him. He was three times my size. He began to walk down the stairs.

All the gifts begin to sing to the Creator. Ando have never seen such a thing. *All things worship the Creator, not just them,* he thought.

The song the gifts were singing the words, "Holy, holy, holy is the Creator, Rich in Mercy and Love."

Ando in disbelief just stares at the Creator.

"Go after the Creator, he is the source of your pain. You can fill the hole inside you through revenge. He is the source of which you can obtain your true glory," the Darkness whispers again to Ando.

Ando staring at the Creator furious takes one step and hears, "Father?"

The darkness flees away like a shadow and disappears when exposed to light. Ando knowing that voice, says, "Sando?"

Out from behind a large rock, he appears. He was crouching down. Ando runs over and attempts to touch him but cannot. He is transparent.

"I, I can't touch you. I have been fighting to regain my, I mean your honor," Ando says as he is getting emotional.

"I have been following you Father, but you say scary things, so I hid from you. You talk to yourself. Why do you do that Father?"

All the moments the Darkness spoke to Ando flashed in front of him. In his mind, he began to realize he was speaking to himself. The Darkness was himself; it kept his son away from him, Ando kept his son away from him.

Ando on his knees is speechless to his son. He takes a deep breath and closes his eyes. He puts his head down and drops his sword. He knows no amount of evil now will fill the hole inside him. He knows revenge is not the answer. But forgiveness.

Ando says, "The Creator is rich in mercy, forgive me."

Sando grabs Ando's hand, to Ando's shock. Sando says with a smile, "Let's go Father."

In the presence of the Creator, Ando's evil intentions caused his body to decay rapidly. His request for forgiveness was the last words out of his mouth. Ando and his son both walked towards the creator.

They both walk right past Manu and into the bosom of the Creator and disappear.

Manu hears behind him, "We must go with the Creator as well." Manu turns around and it is his father. But Manu also sees an amazing sight.

Behind his father was Udo, her father, another young man, and many more.

"You led all of them to the Creator, Son. Well done," Anu said.

All of them walked towards the creator and disappeared into his presence as well.

The Creator turns around as if to leave and Manu says, "What about me? What shall I do now?"

The Creator walked towards Manu and he kneeled before him. He gets close and places his hand on Manu's shoulder. A flash happened and his whole life flashed before his eyes, but it wasn't through Manu's eyes. It was from a third-party perspective.

"Thou good and faithful servant. I have watched thee all thy life. I will establish a new covenant with you. Write down what ye saw today. I am rich and full of mercy. Tell the story of what happened here to avoid it happening again."

Then the Creator raised his hand and the power sword, and the protection sword went to the center of the cavern and into the ground.

"I will leave both swords here and you and only you can remove them from Divine Mountain. This decision I leave to you in my abundance of love."

A flash occurred and the Creator was gone. I fell into exhaustion of my physical body simply in the presence of the Creator. When Manu woke up two members of the Spirit Tribe stood over him.

When Manu sat up both members kneeled before him and held their heads down.

He stood up and awkwardly asked, "Are you two, ok?"

They responded, "You have been touched by the Creator; you have spoken to him in the Cavern of gift inside of Divine Mountain. How can we serve you?"

Manu smirked and asked, "Do you have something to write with?"

Manu sat with the two Spirit Tribe members for seven cycles. Giving specific details about what happened with the swords. The Spirit Tribe members were told to write this information like a story. A story to be told for generations.

When the story was complete, Manu stood up on the seventh cycle and said, "I will return home now." The two Spirit Tribe members looked in fear of him leaving.

Manu said, "Don't worry, I will leave the swords here. On the 700th cycle celebration, I will return and show both swords to all the tribes."

10. THE NEW COVENANT

Manu knew the 700th celebration was within fourteen cycles. But he needed to return to his land. Where his father and he worked. Manu felt in his heart a manner of closure existed upon his return.

His walk would take him a few cycles to get home. As he walked out of Divine Mountain, he saw the slain soldiers and Justo, the slain Purple Tribe boy.

As he walked further, he saw many slain tribesmen. He knew this would not be forgotten. He also knew this would be told by each tribe. They would tell their people their individual story.

Manu knew the covenants were established and to be followed. To follow them was to observe them, working together with each tribe produced a harmony in Chromaria.

But as he saw the massacre of the tribes on his trip home, he knew how important the new covenant was to Chromaria. Manu stopped on his walk through the Dark Woods and looked in both of his hands. He didn't have the sword with him.

Manu realized he was all alone now. His father was gone, his sword with the protective energy was gone and now knowing the Creator was always with him, he watched him disappear.

He felt this was such a monumental task for himself. How was he supposed to be able to tell all the tribes? How could he bring all the tribes together in harmony again?

Manu put his hands to his side and kept walking. He then stopped and thought of the vision the Creator gave him when he touched his shoulder. Manu looked over to his shoulder and he saw something under his shirt. He pulled away his shirt to expose his shoulder and it shined. His shoulder was like a gemstone!

Manu's heart dropped out of shock. He touched it to make sure it was real, and it was a part of his skin now. Manu thought to himself, *this is something I can show the tribes to show my statements are genuine.*

In better spirits he began to hustle home. Upon his arrival he walked over and saw three of his tribesmen waiting. They were standing in the same spot his father died. But his father's body was gone. Manu was reminded of how he ran and didn't perform the covenant for his father upon his death.

He runs up to the three and asks, "Why are you here?"

One of them responded. "We heard your story and came here to find your father. We took him and buried him by the large tree in the midst."

They then stated, "We thought when you returned, you would perform the covenant for his burial." Manu remembered the glorious scene in the Cavern of Gifts where all the trapped spirits returned to the Creator.

He thought to himself, *why would I do this now when I know he has returned to the Creator?* However, Manu realized how blessed he was to observe such an event.

He also recognized how special that moment really was for anyone to witness, including himself. He agreed with the tribesmen and stated, "Walk with me to his burial."

He walked to his father's burial. As he saw the location all of his emotions of everything came back to him. He saw his life taken; he saw him as a spirit following him on his journey. He saw him as he raised his sword and finally, he saw him walk with the Creator.

He kneeled to the grave site. He looked back at the tribesmen and said, "I need a prick of his blood, but you already buried him."

One of the men responded, "I have his shirt, it was stained in his blood." He handed it to Manu. Manu became emotional with a tear coming down one of his eyes.

Manu closed his eyes and said, "Creator in your abundance of love and rich in mercy, please let this tribesman return to his color above with you."

When he did this the three men were startled. Manu's shoulder glowed for a moment after he stated the covenant. They saw it from underneath his shirt.

Manu stood up and told the three men, "The Creator has selected you three for a very important task." The three men looked confused at first but were curious of Manu's next words.

"Now we have eleven cycles remaining until the 700th cycle. This is the most important celebration. You must go to all the tribes, bury their tribesmen. Have them bring an article of their clothing," Manu pauses, "with their blood stain."

The men looked at each other and then back at Manu.

"We will do this," they said.

Manu replied, "Your Creator is rich in mercy, hurry there is no time to waste."

The three tribesmen spread to all the land. Giving the information from Manu and explaining what they must do for the gifts this year at the 700th celebration.

After ten days on his farm, Manu awoke and knew he had a long journey ahead to Mount Divine. He walked outside and two Leaders of the Red Tribe were there. Manu inquired, "Hello, how can I help you?"

The men smiled and didn't say anything. One whistled and out of the field came the most beautiful green beast.

Manu fell in love at first sight, he had never seen such a majestic creator.

The beast ran up to one of the leaders and sniffed his head. The leader smiled and petted the beast. The leader looked at Manu and said, "The Creator is rich in mercy. This is our gift to you; you will ride the beast to Mount Divine. To get on the beast, you only need to give it a name."

Manu walks up to the beast and says, "I will name him Forza." The beast lowered his head then his body for Manu to get on. Manu gets on the beast. The beast raises him up and Manu says to the tribe leaders, "See you at Divine Mountain!"

As Manu traveled through Chromaria he saw all the tribes traveling to Mount Divine. He put his fist up when he saw the crowds and yelled at them, "Chromaria!"

When he arrived many were waiting, the beast behaved nervously seeing all the people, but Manu touched him and whispered that everything was alright.

Manu dismounted off the beast and took his shirt off so everyone could see his shoulder. Many were in awe and whispered amongst each other. He walked by many of the tribesmen. Many were holding articles of clothing. All the tribes in one place each holding their own pain was felt by Manu.

Now he knew the importance of all things the Creator told him to do. It was not simply a manner of just writing these things down. Manu knew the Spirit Tribe would take care of this. But what was done for this celebration would in fact establish the new fourth covenant.

Manu looked around and stated to all the tribes, "Bring your clothing here at the foot of the mountain. I will go up the mountain and return with the two gifts our Creator left us."

As the tribes were instructed, they put all the clothing from their lost loved ones into a pile.

Manu returned down the mountain with both swords in hand. He walked up to the pile of clothing and put both swords into the pile. Then said, "Creator in your abundance of love and rich in mercy, please let this tribesman return to his color above with you."

His shoulder glowed bright as the creator himself when he saw him. He grabbed and held up both swords and said to all the tribes, "Remember the covenants, remember the conflict, and above all else remember our Creator is rich and full of mercy." It is finished and the new covenant was established.

THE END

THE BLUE TRIBE – THE STORY OF UDO

Life was given to the waters by The Creator during the beginning of Chromaria. When the Creator said, "Let the waters have life," a great crystal was set in the center of Chromaria. A giant geyser burst from where the crystal was placed. The waters surged with boisterous merriment. The waters flowed to all areas of the land. It took many forms, such as ice, dew on leaves, and even evaporating to become clouds.

The waters found homes in lakes, streams, rivers, waterfalls, and the sea which surrounded Chromaria. When the Creator was done completing the Water Tribe; two tribe members were originally created from it. Two of the tribesmen were named by the Creator himself: Mizu and Maji. The two were awakened out of the slumber at the mouth of the river flowing from the crystal.

The two rose and greeted each other. Mizu and Maji spoke about what they were dreaming before waking up at the mouth of the river.

Mizu said, "A delta exists on this river, and we must go there, together."

Then Maji replied, "Yes, I had a dream prior to waking up as well. We must follow this river back to its origin."

Maji and Mizu walked a great distance next to the riverbank. Both men felt a connection to the water. Maji put his hand in the water and said, "I can feel others."

Muzi replied, "Others? Like us?"

Maji said, "I believe so, but does this land have others who are not like us?"

The two tribesmen became more confused about their existence as they walked alone.

When they reached the Delta, they noticed a large stone, which caused the river to divert in two different directions. As they got closer, a flash of light occurred. It caused the two men to become frightened. They jumped into the river like a blanket of comfort. The two put their heads underwater to have their bodies fully emerge.

A voice spoke to them while underwater saying, "Ye have found the Great Delta together from the mouth of the river. This Delta is a symbol of what my hands have created, and the responsibility given to your tribe. Thou will continue your journey. This is where you will connect your purpose. I am rich in mercy and consider the waters to be a representation of an outpouring of my limitless love for you. Ye are not alone; you must find the remaining of your tribe. Follow the river until you reach a great expanse of water."

A flash occurred again, and the Creator was gone. Maji and Mizu step out of the river and stand on the riverbank.

Maji spoke, "The voice we heard must be our Creator. He spoke to us as if he was giving us dominion over the water from which we awaken."

Mizu replied, "I agree and believe now we must listen to him. We should continue forward to find the great expanse of water he mentioned."

Maji looked around and then down the river. He said, "We came from the mouth of the river. It was flowing to an expanse of water. Should we go back where we came from?"

Mizu pondered this question. He thought deeply while Maji's interest in Mizu's response grew.

Mizu exhaled and said, "We became aware of ourselves there. Then we travelled to this location, and the Creator spoke to us. We should continue up the river because that was where we were heading."

Maji agreed but was not fully confident in the answer. He suggested, "Well, the Delta causes the river to split. We walked up the river to the Delta. Should we follow the other way back down? The water is flowing towards the Delta. Then it splits and flows down."

Mizu nodded his head in agreement but then said, "This is true, but we should walk to the source rather than the final destination."

So Maji finally agreed and the two continued walking up the river. During their walk they felt something inside their chests. They both stopped and looked at each other.

With one hand on his chest, Muzi asked, "Why do I feel this way?"

Maji took a deep breath and said, "It is a sign we are heading in the right direction. Whatever is at the source is calling us, from the inside. Are we more than just the being that stepped out of the water?"

"We should only focus on our destination. From there, we will learn and know all things," said Mizu.

As they walked, they noticed a waterfall. They knew they would have to climb up a cliff. This was daunting because the size of the waterfall was quite grand.

Mizu said, "This might seem difficult but if we work together, we will reach the top."

Maji agreed and spoke, "I will start, follow me." He grabbed the first area he could on the cliff and climbed to a safe spot. He looked down and instructed, "Come the way I am walking."

Mizu followed Maji all the way to the top. When Maji had reached the top first, he looked all around. He was the first to see all Chromaria from such a high place. He looked behind him and saw something so beautiful.

Maji yelled, "Help me. I am almost up!"

Mizu went to assist and whispered to Maji, "Wait till you see this."

When they both reached the top of the cliff, Maji looked over all of Chromaria; he was in awe.

Muzi put his hand on his shoulder and said, "Look over this way now."

Maji turned around and there was a great expanse of water. In the center of the water was a glowing light.

The two ran towards the lake but stopped suddenly. Mizu and Maji saw one being standing in the water about knee-high. They walked closer. When they got close enough, they saw a tribesperson. The two tribesmen knew it was different but did not understand the differences.

Mizu said, "We should make a promise to the Creator here."

Maji agreed and added, "Let us all hold hands and make a promise."

The three created a circle and held hands. Mizu began to speak with his eyes closed, "Creator, we are grateful for our existence. We thank you for helping us find this tribesperson. We know it is different from Maji and I but we will trust in your limitless love."

Maji then began to speak, "Creator, as a show of our faith, we will all go to the center of the lake together and touch the crystal. It will create our bond. Then we will name the lake, 'The Lake of Promises.'"

After this promise, the three looked over and saw another tribesperson. The three went over to it, and Maji said, "Maybe we should hold hands again and make a promise." The three grabbed the new tribesperson's hand but it felt different.

Mizu said, "Maybe it should just be us two and the new tribesperson." Maji, and Mizu grabbed its hand and stated the promise again. Then they looked at the lake.

The crystal was large and sticking out of the water in the middle of the lake. All four of them swam together to the center: Mizu, Maji, and the two new tribesperson put their right hand on the crystal. Once they all did this, a great light appeared and out of instinct, all four put their full bodies underwater.

The Creator presented himself and spoke again to all of three tribe members, "Well done, thou good and faithful tribesmen. Thou has been faithful over my commands; I will make thee a blessing to my covenants. First these are tribeswomen, and both have much value for your tribe. Take care of them at all costs. Also, ye will split into two groups. Mizu will take one and Maji will take second. The kingdom I give you will spread and flow like my limitless love all through Chromaria, your home.

"Go and grow abundantly. I accept your promise at this lake and will give you another gift. Your bond will extend to each other, and then as generations grow and expand, a deeper bond will penetrate to your soul. Finally, The Great Bond will be sought after for all days that I freely give you. I will put something in the sky. This is where your soul will return when you have had your last cycle. Trust in me as I will trust in you."

Then the light went away, and the Creator was gone. All of them swam to shore. Mizu and Maji went and spoke alone.

Maji said, "Where will each of us go?"

Mizu replied, "We need to split up to honor The Creator. We must also stay close to the water."

Maji thought for a second and suggested, "You can stay here, near the crystal. I will go to the Delta. The Delta was where we first saw the Creator. We will grow our tribe and honor him."

They locked hands and hugged, and then Maji took his tribeswoman and left.

As the beginning continued, the Blue Tribe learned about the covenants and how to honor them. They marvelled at the rainbow in the sky, the other tribes, and the balance between them and the other tribes.

This was the creation and the First Family of the Blue Tribe.